Tina's Diner

JoAnn Adinolfi

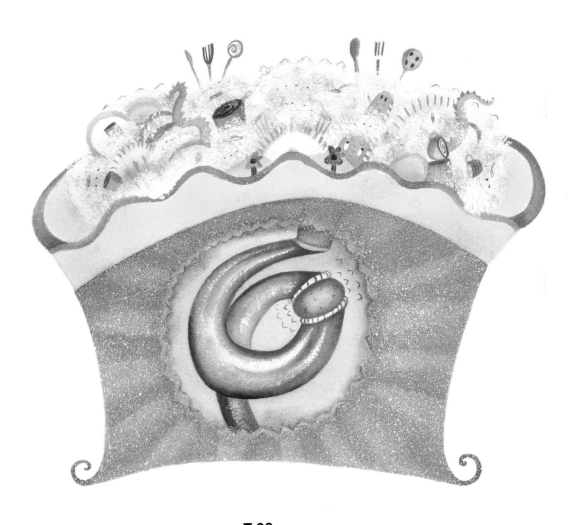

T 98

Simon & Schuster Books for Young Readers

SIMON & SCHUSTER BOOKS FOR YOUNG READERS
An imprint of Simon & Schuster Children's Publishing Division
1230 Avenue of the Americas, New York, New York 10020
Copyright © 1997 by JoAnn Adinolfi.
All rights reserved including the right of reproduction in whole or in part in any form.
SIMON & SCHUSTER BOOKS FOR YOUNG READERS is a trademark of Simon & Schuster.
Book design by Paul Zakris. The text for this book is set in 15-point Berkeley Book.
The illustrations are rendered in gouache, watercolors, pastels, and pastel pencils.
Printed and bound in Hong Kong by South China Printing Company (1988) Ltd.
First Edition
10 9 8 7 6 5 4 3 2 1
Library of Congress Cataloging-in-Publication Data
Adinolfi, JoAnn.
    Tina's Diner / by JoAnn Adinolfi. — 1st ed.
        p.   cm.
    Summary: When the clogged sink at Tina's Diner creates an
    emergency situation and the plumber is out on another job, a
    young customer takes matters into his own hands.
    ISBN 0-689-80634-5
    [Plumbing—Fiction. 2. Diners (Restaurants)—Fiction.
    3. Restaurants—Fiction.] I. Title.
    PZ7.A26115Ti 1997
    [E]—dc20 96-7405

For Dad, with all my heart
Special thanks to Tina,
my hometown, Virginia, and Paul
—J. A.

In Tina's small diner things always ran smoothly.
The hamburgers were always big and juicy,
the pancakes were always fluffier than pillows,

and the ketchup never got stuck in the bottles. Morning, noon, and night, day after day, month after month, year after year, nothing ever went wrong. Until . . .

... the day the sink got clogged.

"Mighty macaroni," said Tina. "In the blink of a burrito I'll be up to my icing in dishes. Hand me the phone. I've got to call J. P. Pettifog, the best plumber in New York City."

Tina buzzed J. P. Pettifog.
She heard,

**"You've reached J. P. Pettifog,
the best plumber in town,
fixing disasters before you
drown. If your water is knee
deep, please leave a message
after the beep."**

"Jumping jelly. It's a machine," complained Tina,
and she left a message, too. "We need your help.
We don't know what to do. Dial 000-2222."

People packed into the small diner hungry for
Tina's yummy food. Tina buttered bagels,
toasted bread, sliced pot roast, scrambled eggs,
scooped potato salad, and sizzled bacon.
The dishes started to pile.
        And pile.
        And pile.

"I'm in deep guacamole," said Tina,

and she rang Pettifog again.

She heard, **"You've reached J. P. Pettifog, the best plumber in town, fixing disasters before you drown. If your water is knee deep, please leave a message after the beep."**

Tina yelled into the phone, "We can't wash a dish, not a fork, not a spoon, the dishes are piling up to the moon! We need your help! We don't know what to do! Dial 000-2222!"

Jeepers, I thought. Tina needs help. She's running out of dishes. Double jeepers, I thought. That means there won't be a supercolossal bowl and spoon for my supercolossal banana skyscraper sundae. This was an emergency. Something had to be done. In a flash, I left to go find the best plumber in town myself.

Which was not going to be easy.

J. P. Pettifog could be working anywhere.

But where?

There!

As we neared the docks, I heard a *clickety-clack tap, bang, clankety-rap* ringing high above the huge, bustling city.

I followed the *clickety-clack tap, bang, clankety-rap* of J. P.'s tools
thwacking against the metal pipes and scrambled toward the roof
of the noisy building. I ran as fast as I could but I was too late. J. P.
Pettifog leaped from the top of the building and parachuted onto a
pagoda in Chinatown.
"Wait for me!"
I shouted and hopped a helicopter uptown.

I dashed through the pagoda's loopy pipes. J. P. Pettifog was just ahead.
Clickety-clack tap, bang, clankety-rap. I stuck close but I was too late.
J. P. sprang on a skateboard and sped away.
"Wait for me!"
I cried as we darted through traffic to a swirly, twirly museum.

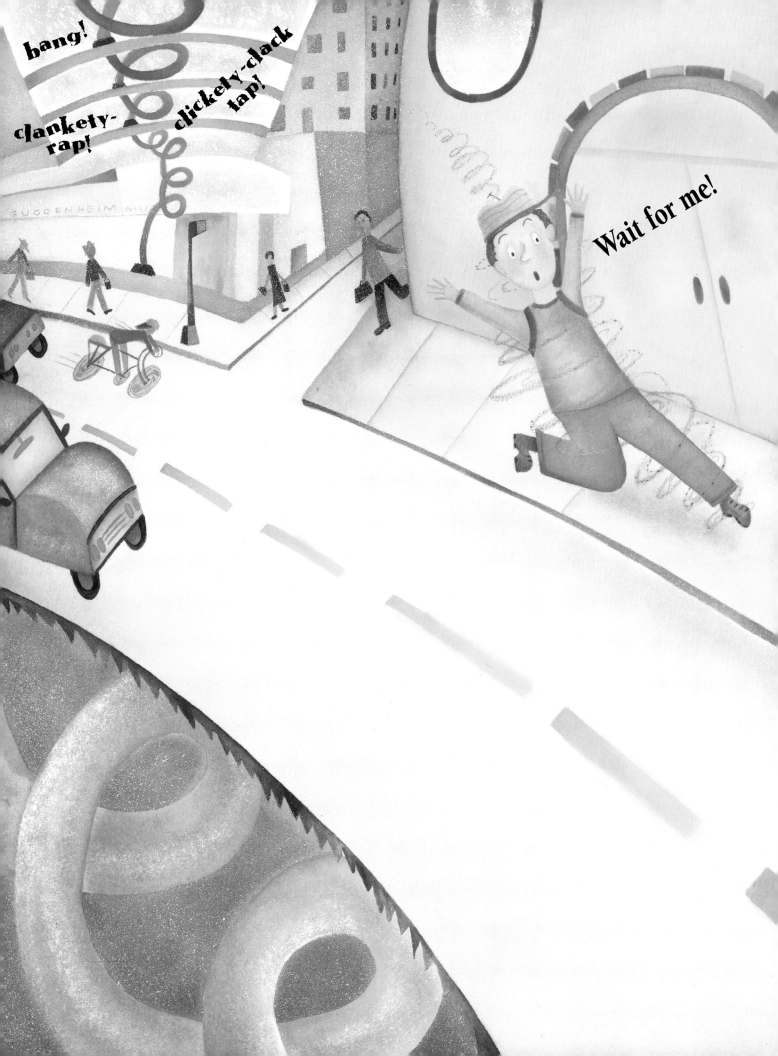

The museum's pipes spun 'round and 'round and 'round.
J. P. Pettifog was just ahead. *Clickety-clack tap, bang,*
clankety-rap. I tried to stick close but I got so dizzy
my eyes crossed. Once again, I was too late.
J. P. was already zooming down the street.
"Wait for me!"
I hollered. All of a sudden, J. P. Pettifog
disappeared into the ground.

Screeeeeech!

I leaned over and asked, "J. P. Pettifog. Are you down there?" I leaned over a little more and asked, "J. P. Pettifog. Where are you?"

I stopped short. My knees were wobbly and I couldn't breathe. "There is no way I am going down there," I thought. "Unh uh. No way."

And then I leaned over a bit too much
and found myself sliding and slipping
into the ooze of the sewer.
It was slimy.
It was smelly.
It was gooey
and it was full of alligators . . .

. . . helping J. P. Pettifog fix a leak.

"Did you call me?" J. P. Pettifog asked.

"I-I-I-I-I did," I stammered. "We need you at Tina's Diner. The sink drain must be fixed."

"I know Tina's," she said. "That's no place for a clogged drain. Let's go."

We sped off in a taxi,

floated away with the ferry,

chugged along by train,

and skated our way to · · ·

. . . Tina's Diner, where things were much worse than we expected.
"Flying french fries!" cried Tina. "It's J. P. Pettifog! Quick! There's not a marshmallow to spare. I am down to my last plate!"

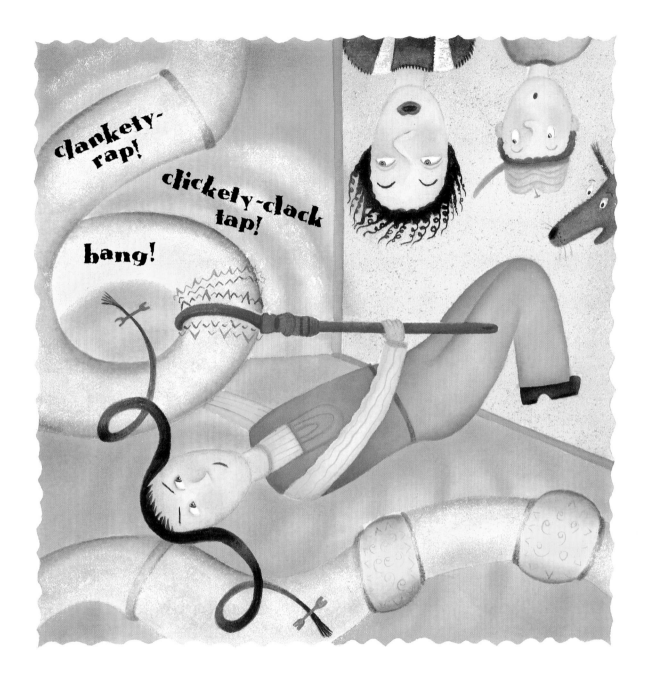

Clickety-clack tap, bang, clankety-rap. J. P. Pettifog, the best plumber in town, hammered and wrenched, banged, clanked, twisted and finally fixed the clogged sink. The water gurgled and burped as it swished through the pipes.

"Let's hit the suds," said Tina.
We piled the dirty dishes into the sink and scrubbed all of
the plates, spoons, forks and knives, cups and saucers,
glasses and bowls until they sparkled.
And when we finished, Tina whipped up two
supercolossal banana skyscraper sundaes
and said, "Thank you for getting me out of
a pickle. You saved my diner."
"It was a piece of cake," said J. P. Pettifog and I.

We dug our nice, clean spoons into our supercolossal rewards and were happy to know that everything was once again running smoothly at Tina's Diner.

Or was it?